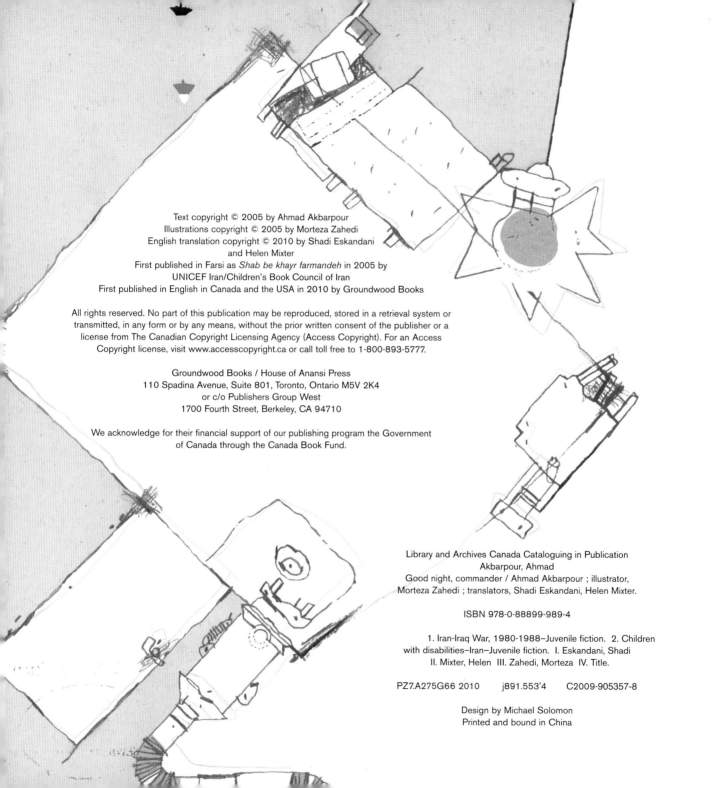

Text copyright © 2005 by Ahmad Akbarpour
Illustrations copyright © 2005 by Morteza Zahedi
English translation copyright © 2010 by Shadi Eskandani
and Helen Mixter
First published in Farsi as *Shab be khayr farmandeh* in 2005 by
UNICEF Iran/Children's Book Council of Iran
First published in English in Canada and the USA in 2010 by Groundwood Books

Groundwood Books / House of Anansi Press
110 Spadina Avenue, Suite 801, Toronto, Ontario M5V 2K4
or c/o Publishers Group West
1700 Fourth Street, Berkeley, CA 94710

We acknowledge for their financial support of our publishing program the Government
of Canada through the Canada Book Fund.

Library and Archives Canada Cataloguing in Publication
Akbarpour, Ahmad
Good night, commander / Ahmad Akbarpour ; illustrator,
Morteza Zahedi ; translators, Shadi Eskandani, Helen Mixter.

ISBN 978-0-88899-989-4

1. Iran-Iraq War, 1980-1988–Juvenile fiction. 2. Children
with disabilities–Iran–Juvenile fiction. I. Eskandani, Shadi
II. Mixter, Helen III. Zahedi, Morteza IV. Title.

PZ7.A275G66 2010   j891.553'4   C2009-905357-8

Design by Michael Solomon
Printed and bound in China

Good Night, Commander

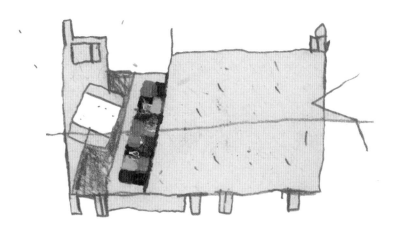

Ahmad Akbarpour   PICTURES BY Morteza Zahedi

Translated by Shadi Eskandani and Helen Mixter

GROUNDWOOD BOOKS   HOUSE OF ANANSI PRESS   TORONTO   BERKELEY

The Iran-Iraq War

A terrible war was fought between Iran and Iraq between 1980 and 1988. A million and a half people died and many more were injured. Many of the dead and injured were innocent civilians. Cities were bombed and Iraq even used chemical weapons.

This long war and the immense suffering it caused a generation of people did not get much attention in the rest of the world. For one thing, it was fought between two countries that were not "popular" in the West. Iran was regarded as a theocratic dictatorship, and Iraq was ruled by Saddam Hussein, a military dictator. But this did not prevent powerful countries in all parts of the world from supporting the war through the secret sales of weapons and other forms of clandestine support.

As always in wars such as these, innocent people — especially children, families, poor people, and soldiers who were forced to fight — were the greatest victims. This story tells us about one such child, his mother and family. His mother died, he lost his leg, and now his father is about to remarry. The story is set in Iran. But it could be the story of any child in any country where a war is fought for economic, strategic, ideological or other reasons, and in the end leaves everyone far worse off than they were before, especially the innocent victims.

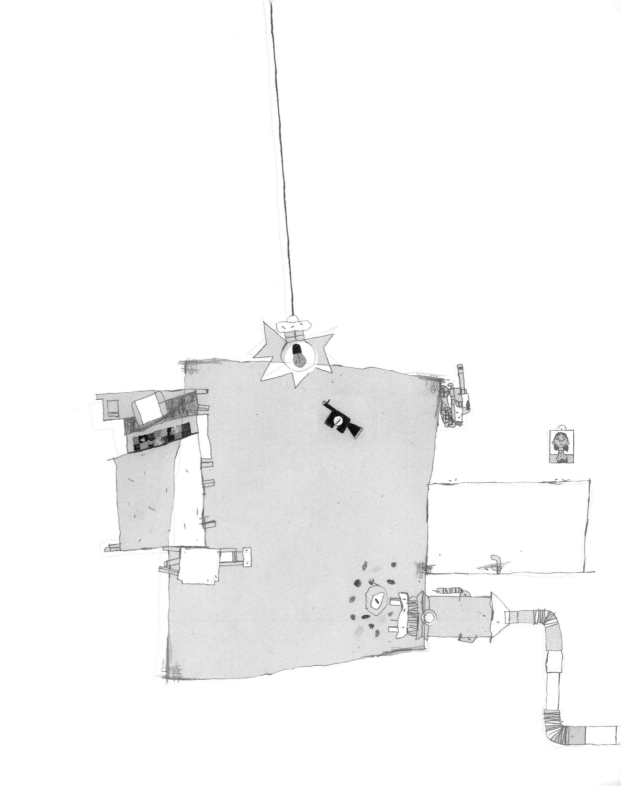

"Hey! Enemy! I'm going to get you with my gun."

Father knocks on the door and comes in.

"I've told you before. You should take off your leg when you are in the house. It makes a lot of noise and you might damage it. Put it over there by the bed," he says.

But I don't want to. How can I fight on one leg? My enemy will just laugh at me.

My father says, "Here, I'll hold your gun while you take it off. Good boy."

I slowly open the two large clasps, then the two smaller ones and undo the strap.

"Good for you," says Father. And he props my leg up against the bed.

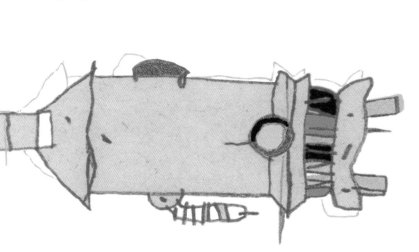

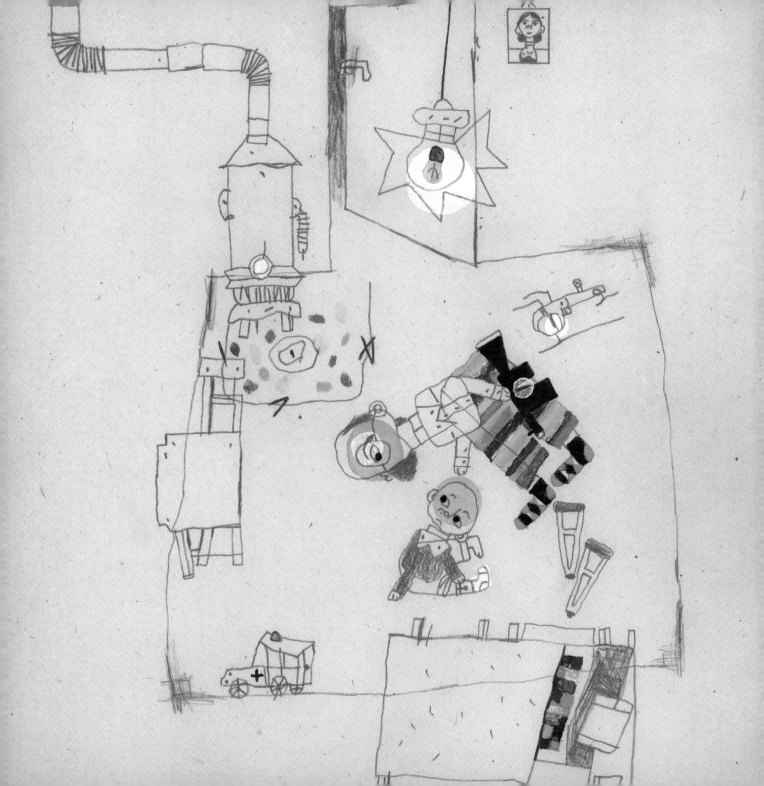

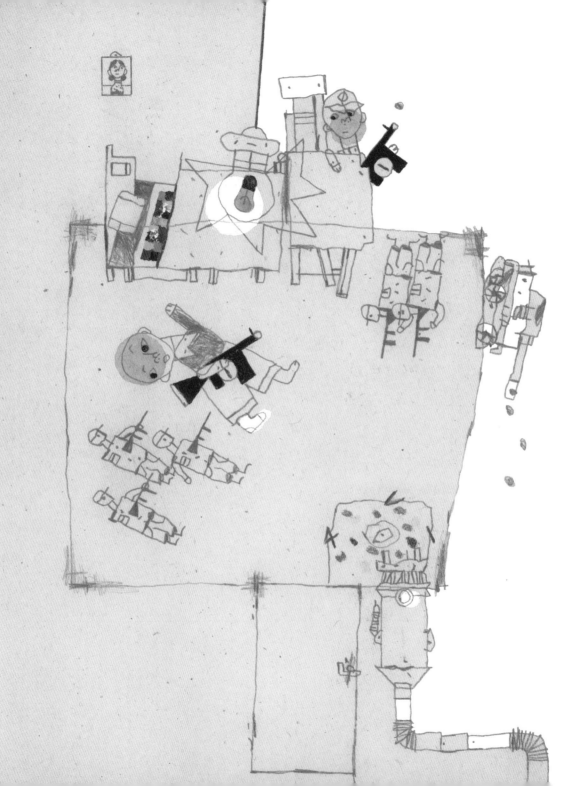

As soon as he leaves I grab my leg and climb under the covers. I don't want the enemy to see me like this. Quickly I shut the two small clasps, then the two big ones and pull the strap up over my back.

Then I jump out of bed and grab my gun.

"Mom, I will avenge your death!" I yell.

My mother in the picture answers, "Be careful."

Now I line up my soldiers on my side of the room. The enemy is on the other side with his.

I am the Commander.

"Get ready!" I order.

"Ay, ay, sir," they reply.

We creep across the battlefield. We have to be brave because there are so many bombs and tanks, maybe even a land mine. If we aren't careful, we could die before we even get to say ouch.

"Attack! Now!" I order and lead the assault. The enemy shoots, but nothing can stop us.

Grenades go off and the room fills with smoke, just like in a movie.

The dark is scary, but I'm not afraid of the dark.

"Right, Mom? When we had to hide in the basement and all the other children were crying and screaming because of the bombs, I just sat next to you and covered my ears with my hands. Remember?"

My mother in the picture says, "That's right, son."

One of my soldiers screams, "I've been hit. I've been hit!"

But I'm the Commander. I don't get scared. I make my way down the hill. Even though my leg hurts, I find the soldier. And I order the troops to stay back.

Then I hear my father calling, "It's time for dinner. Your uncles and aunties are here."

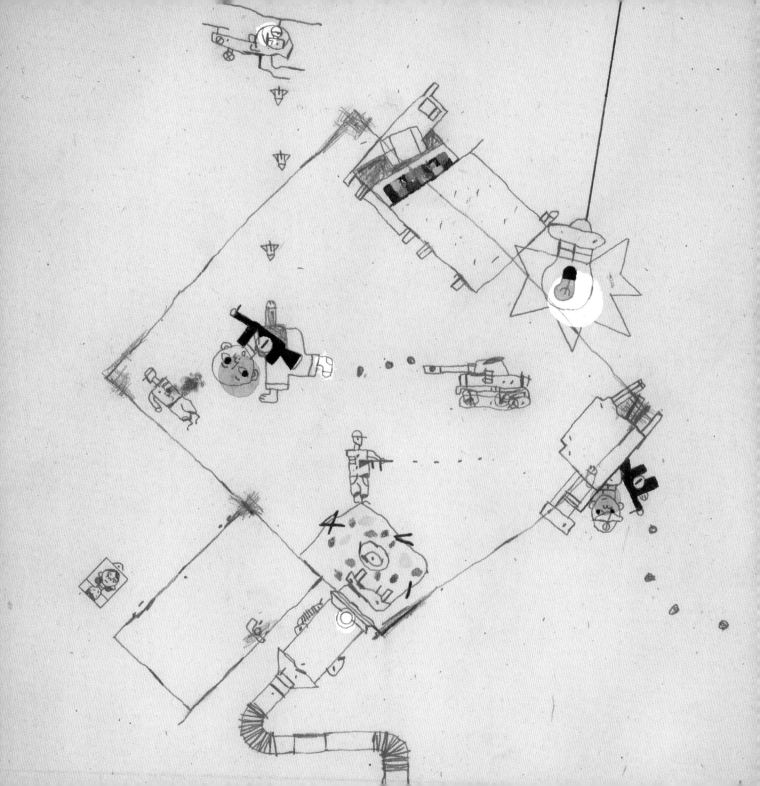

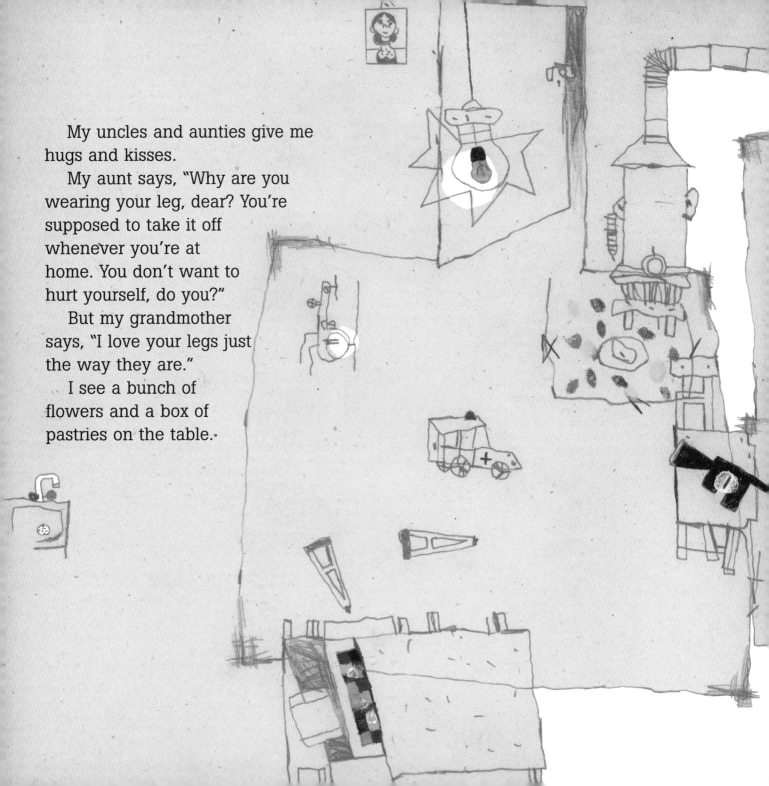

My uncles and aunties give me hugs and kisses.

My aunt says, "Why are you wearing your leg, dear? You're supposed to take it off whenever you're at home. You don't want to hurt yourself, do you?"

But my grandmother says, "I love your legs just the way they are."

I see a bunch of flowers and a box of pastries on the table.

I know why.

My uncle says, "Tonight is a special night. We are going to go and meet your new mother after supper."

I eat as fast as I can and go back to my room.

Everyone leaves the house, except my grandmother.

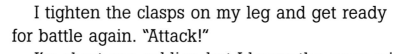

I tighten the clasps on my leg and get ready
for battle again. "Attack!"

I'm short one soldier, but I know the enemy isn't
expecting us and it will be easy to trick him.

The enemy commander is behind the chair. My
leg bangs on rocks and pieces of metal and it hurts.
But nothing can stop me. I'm very close now.

I crawl under the barbed wire and…

"Stop. Don't move. Coward!" I shout as I point
my gun in his face.

He drops his gun so fast and puts his hands up
in the air.

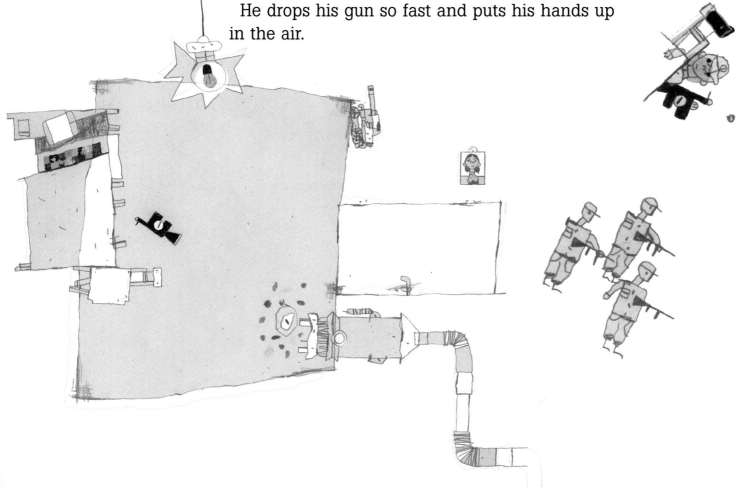

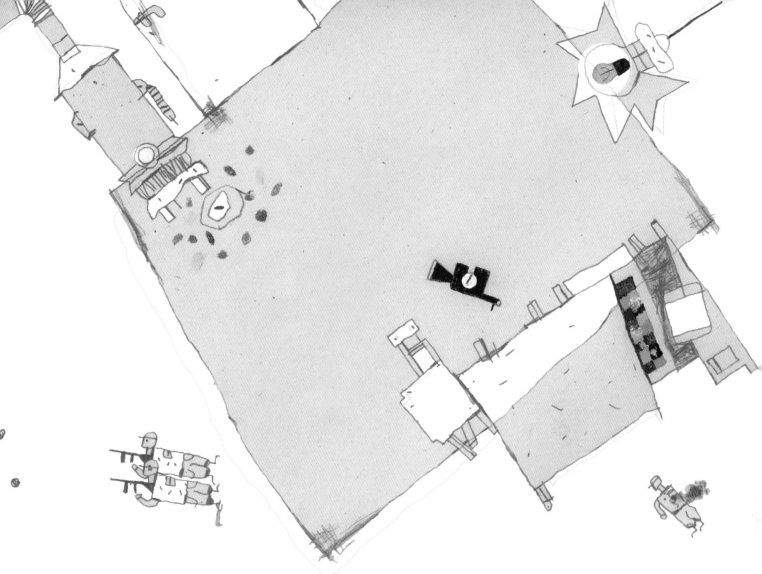

"Tell me right now. Right now! Why did you kill my mother?" I yell.
He starts to cry and says, "I didn't kill your mother. I've just joined up."
     I start to laugh. He is kind of little, maybe even younger than
     me. Or maybe he just looks little because he's so afraid.
      He has a crutch under one arm.
     "Look, I'm here to avenge my mother," I say.
He drops his crutch and grabs his gun. "Me too," he answers back.

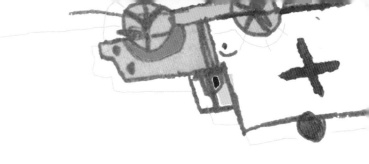

My heart beats really fast. It's my fault. I let him take charge. But I say, "If you don't drop your gun, I'll shoot."

He stops crying. "If you don't drop your gun, I'll shoot," he says and begins to count.

I stare at him and take aim as I count one, two...

But then I see that one of his legs is missing. He's kind of shaking but he's holding himself up on his crutch, and his gun is still pointing right at me.

"Are you missing a leg, too?" I ask.

He's mad. "Don't make fun of me. I'll show you," he says as his finger moves up to the trigger.

I say, "Look, look."

I drop my gun and roll up my pant leg. I open the large clasps, then the small clasps, undo the strap and take off my leg.

Then I hop over and pick up my crutches. He can't believe it. He drops his gun and picks up my leg.

"Can you walk with this?" he asks.

"Yes," I say.

"Can you run?"

"Yes."

I reach down and roll up his pants and put my leg on the ball of his knee. I close the large clasps, then the smaller ones and do up the strap.

He runs around the chair. "Can I borrow this, just for tonight? I want to show my mom."

"I thought she was dead," I say.

"Yes, but she can see me."

"Okay, but only for tonight," I say.

"I promise." And he disappears behind the chair.

Our soldiers are still fighting.

"Cease-fire, cease-fire," I call.

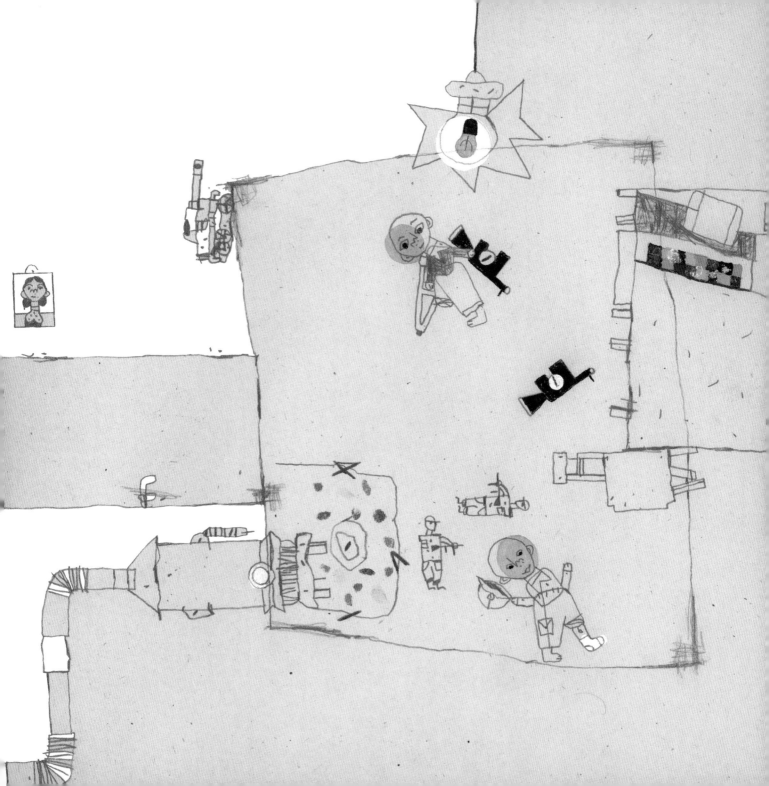

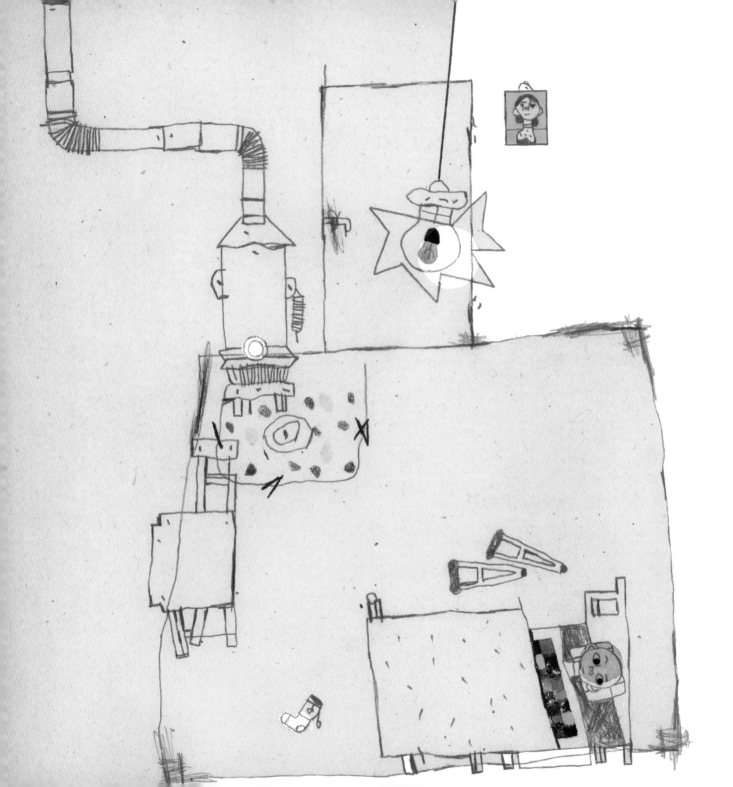

I am ashamed to look over at my mother.
I promised I would avenge her and I didn't.

Then I hear her say, "Congratulations, Commander. I'm proud of you."

I climb into bed. I don't want a new mother. I look at my mother in the picture. She is crying.

"Don't cause trouble for your father," she says.

He hasn't come home yet.

I don't answer. I pull the covers up around my shoulders.

But then I hear my mother in the picture
say, "Good night, Commander. Sleep tight."